CLYDE AND HIS NEW FRIENDS

By
Mike Zane

Dedication

As a first time writer I had much needed support from Kristy, my wife of 50 years. She is a retired school teacher and took it upon herself to correct all my punctuation and sentence structure mistakes. Thanks to P.T Deutermann, retired Navy Captain who gave me permission to use the name Grace Ellen Snow from one of his best selling books. Thanks to Sasha Barber and her team at LT—WRITING. As product manger, she and her team guided the production of the book from start to finish.

CLYDE AND HIS NEW FRIENDS

It wasn't the night before Christmas, but mice were certainly stirring. Once upon a time there was a tiny house mouse named Clyde. Clyde lived with his mother in a big empty house on a high hill. Clyde's house was a tiny hole in a wall in the empty house. The hole in the wall was so small that it was tough to see.

Every day Clyde's mother would leave their little hole in the wall to go outside to find food for them. Since no one lived there except Clyde and his mother, there was no food to be had there. While his mother was looking for food, Clyde only wandered through the big house in the day time. He used to have fun running up and down the stairs. He always looked for the piece of paper that he found when he was younger. He would run and jump on the paper and slide across the wooden floor like a giant slide. He wondered where that paper had gone, but gone it was. The big house always creaked and groaned and made spooky little noises at night. So, all of his exploring was during the day. Every day he looked in all the rooms to see if anything had changed since the last time he looked. He hoped he would find something different or something he could play with. As usual, nothing had changed at all. Clyde didn't know it, but his life would change in ways he couldn't imagine.

One day when Clyde's mother went out to look for food for them, he heard deafening noises outside the little HOLE IN THE WALL door. He heard loud thumping, things dragging across the floor. The loud noises continued all through the house for a long time. Clyde didn't know, but all the noise was caused by furniture and household goods brought into the house by the family moving in. Clyde wanted to look for his mother but was too afraid of all the loud noise, so he stayed inside the little hole in the wall.

While Clyde was waiting for his mother to return and the loud noises to stop, he became tired and sleepy. He soon fell fast asleep dreaming of his mother bringing food back to their little hole in the wall home. When Clyde woke up, he didn't hear anything. It was hushed in the big house. Clyde looked around for his mother. She was not in their little home. He was still afraid of what might be outside of his little door, so he stayed inside and waited and waited for what seemed like a long time. But his mother still did not come home. Clyde thought she might have gotten lost and couldn't find her way home.

Clyde did not know what to do. He wanted his mother, and he was also starving. He was still waiting for his mother when he fell fast asleep again. When he woke up, he heard some shallow sounds outside his door. He peeked out and saw two small girls skipping into the room. They sat down on the floor and opened some books. A new family had moved into the house when Clyde had heard all the loud noises. The girls were Lindsey, age ten and Sarah, age nine. They were dressed almost the same. Lindsey was wearing a bright blue dress with a big bow in front. Her white shoes had something on top that sparkled. Her sister Sarah wore a long red dress that had long pink ribbons hanging from top to bottom. The girls almost always dressed the same, with brightly colored dresses with bows and ribbons. Both girls had long yellow curly hair hanging past their shoulders. They were sitting on the floor coloring in a book. Lindsey was coloring a picture of a mouse.

Even though the two girls were small, they looked very large compared to a small house mouse. Clyde was still hungry for he had not had anything to eat since before his mother left. He thought, "Since I'm small, maybe the girls won't see me, and I can look for food." He slowly came out of the little hole in the wall when Lindsey saw him. She was shocked to see a small mouse. She called to her sister, "Look over there." She pointed to Clyde and said, "See how cute he is. He has very long whiskers and big round ears. He looks just like the picture in my coloring book." Sarah clapped and said, "See if he will come over here." Clyde made a big squeak and started to run back to his little hole in the wall, but Lindsey called to him in a very soft voice. She was not afraid of Clyde. The two girls got down on their knees, and Lindsey held out her hand. Clyde came a little closer and saw no reason to be afraid. Clyde jumped onto her foot and ran up her leg to her outstretched hand. She rubbed Clyde's long whiskers and scratched his big round ears. Sarah ran to the kitchen and found a nice grape. She brought it back to see if Clyde would eat it. By this time Clyde was very hungry and thought this was nice. He made a fine feast of that grape. The girls were surprised and laughed when Clyde stood up on his hind legs and began to clean his long whiskers, for Clyde was a very clean little mouse.

Over the next few days, Clyde thought his mother was not returning. She had never been gone this long. He was sad, because he didn't know what had happened to her. He knew she had gone outside to look for food. He thought again that she had probably gotten lost. Clyde wished very hard and hoped nothing bad had happened to her. Pretty soon, Clyde and the two girls became fast friends. This helped Clyde when he was feeling sad about his mother. One of the girls would bring small tidbits of food for him, so he never got hungry again. One of his favorite foods was grapes. The girls would put his food in a small dish outside his hole in the wall door. The girls learned by watching Clyde and listening to his different eeks and squeaks, they could tell if he was hungry or wanted to play.

Clyde and the girls played games only two girls and a small mouse could play. The girls would hold their arms and hands out and Clyde would run and jump from one girl to the other. Sometimes he would get caught in one of the girl's long yellow curls. Then the girl would have to be extra careful not to hurt Clyde getting him untangled. Lindsey and Sarah had a big doll house that had many rooms. Clyde would play hide and seek with the girls by hiding in different rooms. Since he was small, he could hide, and the girls had difficulty finding him. The girls thought Clyde was funny as he ran in and out of the doll house rooms.

Sometimes when Clyde and the girls were playing, the mother or father would come into the room, Clyde would hide in one of the pockets in the girls dress. He was a small mouse, so he could stay hidden and not make a sound.

Sarah thought Clyde was a wonderful friend and made him a nice bed. She found a small box and put some cotton in to make it soft. Every night Clyde would curl up in the soft cotton and go fast asleep. He thought, "I don't have to worry about a place to live and I won't be hungry anymore."

As time passed, Clyde and the two girls were always together when the girls were home from school. One morning Clyde woke up and washed his whiskers and ears. He went through his little hole in the wall and found the small dish with two grapes. After finishing the grapes, he washed his whiskers carefully, as always. He played by himself running up and down the curtains by the window. It was just a short distance from his door, and he could run very fast and up the curtain to the top, then across and down the other side. He was careful not to harm the curtains. He got tired of playing pretty soon and went inside his hole in the wall door. He thought he would nap and be ready to play with the girls when they came home. Clyde must have been very tired for, he was asleep for a long time. He didn't hear the furniture movers or the people carrying things out of the house. He didn't know the family had suddenly moved out.

When Clyde woke up from his long nap, the house was quiet. He thought this was strange, because the girls would usually be playing in the room where his door was. To his surprise, he entered the room, and all the furniture was gone. He walked all through the house and saw all the rooms were empty. He thought, "Am I going to be alone again?" He found several small pieces of bread left in the kitchen. He did not know the family had moved away. He wondered what his friends, the two girls, were doing now. Did they have another mouse to play with? He carried the pieces of bread to his hole in the wall door. Going inside, he climbed into his soft bed and went to sleep. The house was quiet for several days. He wasn't hungry, because he saved the pieces of bread and only ate when hungry. He was still wondering when he would get food again.

The following day he woke up to loud noises in the house again. He thought, "Are the girls coming back?" He told himself, "I'll wait to see after all the noises stop." It was almost a full day before all the noise stopped. And soon it was all quiet in the house. Clyde ventured a peek through his door to see what was happening in the room. He saw a little girl sitting in a chair looking out a window. When he looked closer, he saw the girl was crying. Well, having two young girls for friends before that were always happy and laughing, he didn't understand why the girl was so sad. He didn't know that the girl and her family had moved a long way. He didn't know that the girl was missing all her friends, and that was why she was sad. He saw the girl was dressed in a bright yellow sun dress with yellow flowers all over. She was tall with long black hair and big blue eyes. She was wiping her eyes with a large white handkerchief.

Grace Ellen Snow was ten years old. She just started going to her new school. For several days Clyde saw that sometimes when she came home, she just sat in the chair by the window and looked sad. Sometimes she cried. Clyde didn't know that some of the girls at her school teased her because she was taller than they were, and that made her cry. She wanted them to like her for who she was, not how she looked.

Clyde came out of his hole in the wall door and climbed up the side of the chair where the girl could see him. "Oh," the girl said, "where did you come from? Did you come here to cheer me up?" Clyde stood up on his hind legs, twitched his long whiskers and wiggled his big round ears. This made the girl laugh out loud. She put the handkerchief in her—sun dress pocket and reached out, and Clyde climbed up into the palm of her hand. She said, "What a fine looking mouse you are. I don't have any friends here. Will you be my friend?" She said, "My name is Grace Ellen Snow, and I don't know your name. But I will call you Clyde after a friend from a long time ago." Clyde thought, "I wonder how she knows my name?" Grace put Clyde back on the arm of the chair and said, "I have a cat named Pumpkin. Oh, I don't know if he will like you. I don't think he has ever seen a mouse before." Grace tells Clyde, "Maybe you had better return to your house for now, and I will talk to Pumpkin." Grace named her cat Pumpkin because he was a big orange cat. He had fluffy fur that made him look very soft. Grace knew that orange tabby cats were the most gentle and affectionate of all the cats.

After a while, Grace returned but did not have Pumpkin with her. Grace called Clyde several times before he came out of the hole in the wall door. He looked around to see if the cat named Pumpkin was with Grace. When Clyde did not see the cat, he ran to Grace and jumped into her outstretched hand. Clyde stood up on his hind legs and began smoothing his whiskers and rubbing his mouth. Grace looked puzzled for a minute, and then realized that Clyde was showing he was hungry. Grace put Clyde down on the chair, because she did not want to take him to the kitchen. Grace's mother was fixing lunch for her. Grace did not want her mother to know she had a mouse for a friend.

Grace found a piece of apple and a bit of cheese. She didn't know what mice ate, but thought Clyde might like these tidbits. Returning to the family room, she saw Clyde sitting on the chair, waiting for her. Grace sat down and held out her hand. Clyde jumped down and saw the apple and cheese. Clyde remembered his mother had brought back cheese for him, so he knew he liked it. Clyde finished the cheese and took a small bite of the apple. He thought to himself, "This is as good as the grapes tasted." Grace told Clyde she would bring food for him every day. Grace thought she had two friends now, Pumpkin and Clyde. She would not be so lonely, despite missing her other friends. She thought that most kids had cats and dogs for friends. Some even had birds and lizards. She didn't know anyone that had a mouse for a friend.

Grace found Pumpkin in his favorite place. He always napped in the sun on the window sill by her chair. Grace picked Pumpkin up and sat him in her lap. She told him about Clyde. Pumpkin looked at her with big green eyes and cocked his head to one side as if to say, "What is a mouse?" Grace told him, "Clyde is a small mouse with long whiskers and big round ears. He likes to play and sits on my shoulder. He is my friend, just like you are. Because he is small, you must be careful not to hurt him."

Grace called Clyde to come out and meet Pumpkin. Clyde came out of his hole in the wall door. He saw Grace sitting with Pumpkin. Clyde thought if Pumpkin didn't like him, he was fast enough to return to his door. Grace held her hand down so Clyde could climb up. She held her hand with Clyde in front of Pumpkin. Pumpkin opened his mouth and licked Clyde with one big lick of his big pink tongue. Clyde was covered from his big round ears to his tail with kitty spit. Clyde was surprised and thought he didn't need a bath because he was already clean. Grace giggled and laughed at the sight. Clyde stood up on his hind legs and rubbed his hands over his whiskers, face, and ears to dry them. Pretty soon he was dry enough and hopped onto Pumpkin's back and scratched his ears to show him he didn't mind the wash, and he was Pumpkin's friend.

Over the following days and months, Grace Ellen Snow, Clyde, and Pumpkin became close friends. Grace learned how to tell if Clyde was hungry or wanted to play, because she learned that from watching Pumpkin. She knew when Pumpkin wanted to play or when he wanted food. He made specific meows when he was hungry. He would roll over on his back when he wanted his tummy rubbed. Clyde would stand on his back legs and rub his long whiskers when hungry.

Grace made new friends at her new school, but not as close as Clyde and Pumpkin. When Clyde went to his hole in the wall home, Pumpkin always laid down in front of the door as if to be a guard for Clyde. In the morning when Clyde came out, Pumpkin was there to greet him. Grace decided to bring Pumpkin's bed down from her bedroom and put it next to Clyde's hole in the wall door. Pumpkin's bed also hid the tiny hole in the wall. Grace always put food out for Clyde before she went to school. And it was always in a place where her parents could not see it. Clyde was always surprised of what Sarah left for him to eat. She discovered he liked grapes and tried hard to find some for him. Sometimes Pumpkin would meow softly to let Clyde know he was outside his door. It seemed to Grace that Pumpkin and Clyde would talk to each other with meows and squeaks.

Clyde wondered what became of the two girls who were so friendly and cared for him before Grace Ellen Snow came to live in the house on the hill. He hoped they found another friend to make them as happy as he was. Clyde was always sitting on the chair when Grace came home from school. He jumped to her shoulder sat down and cleaned his long whiskers and round ears. He especially did this before Pumpkin could lick him full of kitty spit. He didn't like being wet, but didn't want to hurt Pumpkin's feelings.

In the afternoon the three would play games. They were always looking to find something new to try. Pumpkin liked to chase a ball to bat around. Clyde tried to catch the ball, but Pumpkin was too fast and always got to it first. Pumpkin tried to let Clyde push the ball, but he was too small to push it very far. Grace thought she could find a small ball for Clyde to play with. She found a blue and white marble in her mother's fish tank. There were enough marbles in the fish tank that one would not be missed. The marble was small enough for Clyde to push around on the floor. Clyde's favorite game was running up and down the window curtains. Grace laughed when Clyde would jump from the curtains down to Pumpkin and onto his back for a ride around the room. Pumpkin and Clyde enjoyed their games while Grace was at school. They had jumping contests to see who could jump the farthest. Clyde could jump pretty far for a mouse, but Pumpkin always won because he was bigger.

Clyde could hide under the sofa, which was too low for Pumpkin when they played hide and seek. Since Pumpkin could jump higher than Clyde, he jumped up and hid atop the big grandfather clock. Once Clyde hid behind a flower pot that was on a table. When Pumpkin walked by, Clyde jumped down right onto Pumpkin's back. It startled Pumpkin, causing him to jump straight up in the air. Clyde flew off Pumpkin's back, did a summersault, and landed on a soft pillow on the sofa. Both were tired of playing, so they went to their favorite place by the window for a nap. When Grace came home from school, she sat in the chair by the window to do school work. Pumpkin and Clyde would nap by the window with the sun warming them. Pumpkin's purring always made Clyde sleepy.

Time passed and Grace Ellen Snow was in middle school. She made new friends and had new activities to keep her busy. She never told any of her friends about Clyde. She knew that most girls would not understand how Clyde helped her when she was sad. Everyone knows cats eat mice, but Pumpkin was different. He liked Clyde, and they were best friends. Pumpkin and Clyde would play together when Grace was at school or out with her parents. Pumpkin liked to nap by the window when the sun came in. Clyde would climb up, lay on Pumpkin's back, and nap too. If anyone came into the room, they couldn't see Clyde nestled in Pumpkin's fluffy fur. She didn't see as much of Pumpkin and Clyde as before, but still made time to play and be with them as much as possible. She always found them in the window with the sun. Pumpkin stretched out with Clyde on his back in his fluffy fur. It was slowly becoming winter, and Christmas was coming soon, and Grace thought she would get something for Clyde and Pumpkin.

She thought about it for a while trying to think of something that would be nice for a mouse and a cat. One day she was shopping with her parents, and saw some small gold and silver chains in the jewelry store window. She couldn't go into the store to buy the chains while she was with her parents. One day, Grace went to the jewelry store after school and bought one small gold chain and one silver chain. She had the jeweler attach a small bell to each chain. December came with the Christmas season. Grace's parents bought a Christmas tree and placed it in the room where Clyde and Pumpkin played. The tree was decorated with ornaments, lights, and tinsel. Boxes covered with bright wrapping paper were placed under the tree. Clyde liked to climb up the tree and play in the branches and ornaments, being careful not to damage any. Pumpkin wanted to walk under the tree and smell the boxes to see if food inside them. On Christmas day after Grace and her parents had celebrated by opening presents and having Christmas dinner. Grace placed the small chains around Clyde and Pumpkin's necks and listened to the small bells when they tinkled. Clyde and Pumpkin had been together now for a long time, and as they were getting older, they didn't play as much as before, but they still took their naps in the window by Grace's chair. Grace came home from shopping with her parents. She looked for Pumpkin and Clyde. Not seeing them, she listened for the tinkle of Pumpkin and Clyde's bells. Not a sound was heard. She went to her chair by the window. There she found Clyde and Pumpkin in their customary place on the window sill in the sun. Both had passed away together sometime during the night. Grace's mother was not surprised that Pumpkin had passed away because he was getting pretty old for a cat, but she was very surprised to see Clyde beside him. Grace told her mother about finding Clyde, and how he had become a friend of hers and Pumpkin. Grace's mother saw the gold and silver chains with the tiny bells and said, "That was so nice for your friends and very thoughtful. That shows how different animals can be lifelong friends like Clyde and Pumpkin, as different people can be lifelong friends. I am so proud of you."

Grace thought about what to do for Clyde and Pumpkin. She told her mother she wanted to make a grave for them in the garden under the widow where they liked to bask in the sun together. Grace's mother asked, "Do you still have that small doll bed when you still played with dolls? I know you gave all your dolls to the children's home, but maybe you still have the bed." Grace looked all through her bedroom and found the little doll bed in her closet. She also found a small pink satin blanket. She thought it would it would make an excellent cover for her friends. She removed the gold and silver chains and placed them in a box on her bedroom dresser. She placed Pumpkin and Clyde side by side in the bed and carefully covered them with the satin blanket.

Grace told her mother she didn't want any help with the grave because they were her friends and she wanted to do everything herself. She found a wooden box that had a top with a handle. She placed the doll bed inside the box and carefully sealed the top. She dug the grave, ensuring it would be deep enough to hold the box. She wanted enough room over the top to plant a lovely rose bush and have room for a little name plaque with the names of her friends and the date when they passed. She took a picture of the grave, plaque, and rose bush. She placed the picture next to the box with the gold and silver chains. Grace Ellen Snow brings out the box with the chains every Christmas and hangs them on her Christmas tree. Each time she walks by, the little bells tinkle once. She knows that Pumpkin and Clyde are still together. She does this every Christmas, even after she gets married and has her own children. When they ask about the picture and the chains, she tells them the story of growing up in the big house on the hill and her friends Clyde and Pumpkin.

Author Bio

As a first time author, it took a long time to write a short children's story. After graduating from high school, I joined the US Army and spent 7 years doing classified electronic intelligence with the Army Security Agency. I'm proud to say I volunteered to be one of the first members of a classified unit sent to South VietNam in 1961. Two months after leaving the army, I joined the Lodi Police Department in 1964. I retired as a sergeant in 1989 after 25 years. During that time I had assignments in defectives, crime scene investigation, lab supervisor, and patrol supervisor. My wife and I have traveled to 30 plus countries. My hobbies are golfing and ham radio. I have been licensed since 1956 while in high school, and my present call is N6ZW. I'm hoping to start a second children's book.